Thirty One Day
MARRIAGE RESET

FORMING HEALTHY HABITS TO ENRICH YOUR MARRIAGE.

BY: ANDREW
& COURTNEY BENJAMIN

Thirty One Day Marriage Reset

ISBN: 9781792123542
Imprint: Independently published

Disclaimer: The content in this devotional are interpretations and opinions of Andrew & Courtney Benjamin based on Biblical principles. We are not licensed professionals. Some circumstances in marriage may need the assistance of professionals or authorities, such as abuse. Please do not hesitate to seek professional help.

Foreword:

Marriage is the most holy, weighty, and wonderful example we have on earth of the covenantal union between Christ and His Bride, the Church. In much of our modern church culture, we insist that there must be some secret strategy to which only the most well-known pastors and leaders are privy, and that, if they would share it with us, we'd be better qualified to help lead people to Jesus. We invest countless millions of dollars into state-of-the-art sound and lighting systems for our church buildings, social media marketing campaigns and website designs, and we obsess about making sure that our leaders are as gifted, well-studied, and well-dressed as possible. But after having spent years on the platform of ministry, I am more convinced than ever before that the most significant testimony we, as a church, can present to an unbelieving world is a healthy family--and a healthy family starts with a healthy marriage. Scripture is full of lessons and stories that reinforce the idea that marriage is God's principal institution in the earth. From the union of Adam and Eve in the Garden of Eden, to the marriage supper of the Lamb in Revelation 19, Yahweh has woven into the pages of His Word a foundation of intimacy, devotion, legacy, and love upon which we can—and must--build the unshakeable marriage that so much of our modern world struggles to even imagine.

From forgiveness to communication, and from devotion to intimacy, we are able to see countless parallels between the intimate, covenantal relationship Christ shares with us, and the intimate, covenantal relationship we can share with our spouse. This means that, if you know the love of God, you have been given an inside track on success in marriage! You can learn to love your husband or wife by beholding the ways that Jesus has loved you.

The simple fact that you are reading this book shows that you're committed to cultivating a strong and God-honoring marriage. And that commitment—coupled with God's Word and God's Spirit at work in you—is a recipe for success. Ultimately, the primary requirement for a wonderful marriage is an unceasing commitment to it. There will be days that you don't feel like putting forth the effort to love your spouse. There will be days that you feel offended, frustrated, or betrayed—and often for justifiable reasons. But the best marriages in the world are built in the shadow of the Cross, which stands to remind us that just as Jesus laid His life down for the sake of love, so also should we. In Thirty One Day Marriage Reset, Andrew and Courtney Benjamin will seek to offer biblical, practical, and personal insight and direction that I believe will strengthen and rejuvenate your marriage, if you will let it. To read the passages contained in this book is one thing, but to prayerfully discuss and apply them is another thing entirely. I want to challenge you to approach this next month with eagerness, passion, and humility. Choose to serve your spouse, to celebrate your marriage, and to tear down any walls you may have built to keep your husband or wife at a distance. Walk this path together, for the good of your marriage, and for the glory of God. My prayer for you over these next thirty-one days is that you might discover new depths of passion in God's heart for your spouse, and that, with God's passion, you might love them in truth, in courage, and in kindness that will carry you onward together as you discover God's best for your lives. There is indescribable glory in a marriage built on the goodness of God, and Thirty One Day Marriage Reset will give you the tools you need to build it.

By: Mattie Montgomery

We dedicate this devotional to our sweet Juanita Callaway.

You mean so much to us and we are bound and determined to set the standard of a Godly Marriage in our home. We will serve one another, be faithful to one another, and love one another all the days of our lives. You have brought a new and another importance to our marriage, and we strive to constantly remember that you are watching and soaking in the way that we treat one another. You are so important to us! We love you, sweet princess!

Love,
Mommy and Daddy

DAY 1

The most guaranteeing way to turn your marriage away from destruction is to choose to turn yourself away from sin.

•••

It is so important in marriage to remember that sin is not just avoiding those big, "no nos." Sin is disobedience, too. It's not just avoiding things like adultery, it is also ignoring the voice and nudges of God. If God whispers for you to hug your spouse and tell them that you love them in the middle of a difficult conversation or disagreement and you refuse, that is sin for you. If God tells you to send a text message saying that you're sorry and your pride gets in the way, that is sin for you. You know Satan would never tell you to be kind and forgiving towards your spouse... so when you feel those prompts, thank God for looking out for your marriage and obey Him.

•••

Submit yourselves, then, to God. Resist the devil, and he will flee from you.
James 4:7 (NIV)

Thoughts and ideas:

_____

_____

_____

_____

_____

_____

_____

_____

_____

_____

_____

_____

_____

_____

_____

_____

_____

_____

_____

DAY 2

If you see a problem in your marriage, you don't stop participating in your marriage, you stop participating in the problem
•••

Sometimes it is easy to draw back and not communicate when we are frustrated with our spouse. It's easy to listen to that little voice telling us, "Well I'm just not going to talk because _____." You fill in the blank. However, speaking up and having those hard conversations is sometimes the key to not having the same frustration about the same situation again. If you need to read 1 Corinthians 13 before approaching your spouse about something that is bothering you, do it. But don't dust it under the rug and hope it cleans itself up. Have the attitude that you will do whatever it takes and have whatever conversation that needs to be had before you allow it to keep your marriage from thriving and being at it's full potential.
•••

Turn from evil and do good; seek peace and pursue it.
Psalm 34:14 (NIV)

Thoughts and ideas:

_____

_____

_____

_____

_____

_____

_____

_____

_____

_____

_____

_____

_____

_____

_____

_____

_____

_____

_____

_____

_____

DAY 3

Do you put effort into being sweet, kind, patient, soft toned, etc.? If not, maybe you should try it today and the rest of your days.

•••

What does your spouse love? Coffee? Tea? Hamburgers? Tacos? Walks? Board games? Take note of those things and go out of your way for them. Fix them a cup of coffee. Take a walk with them. Choose a little something to do that shows them that you care and that your relationship is not based on convenience but rather on the fact that you desire to serve them. Kindness isn't always convenient, but it's always worth it... especially in marriage. Hold hands in the car. Give a kiss when you arrive, another when you're leaving, and many in between. Give a long hug. Give a massage. Be present.

How can you go out of your way to be kind today?

•••

We love because he first loved us.
1 John 4:19 (NIV)

Thoughts and ideas:

_____

_____

_____

_____

_____

_____

_____

_____

_____

_____

_____

_____

_____

_____

_____

_____

_____

_____

_____

_____

DAY 4

The future is a stranger, but if the two of you focus on the One who holds it then neither of you ever have to worry about what it may hold.

•••

Fear... Whew... Fear is such a liar yet is sometimes so easy to believe. It is so easy to freak out when the finances don't amount to the bills. Or when a loved one is really sick. Or when the car breaks down. Or when _____... You fill in the blank. There are so many different circumstances and situations that pull us towards fear. Fear is always trying to creep its way into our lives and into our marriages. However, we serve a God that is far more worthy of our attention and energy than those lies that are trying to cripple us and put strains on our marriages. Today is the day to turn your worry into praise and thank God that you have nothing to worry about. Thank Him that you can literally trust Him with everything and tell Satan that you're not buying his lies.

If fear tries to stress you out today, before you allow it to control you... ask yourself if God is stressed out about it? He isn't. Because He already has a plan.

•••

For I know the plans I have for you", declares the Lord, "plans to prosper you and not to harm you, plans to give you hope and a future.
Jeremiah 29:11 (NIV)

Thoughts and ideas:

_____

_____

_____

_____

_____

_____

_____

_____

_____

_____

_____

_____

_____

_____

_____

_____

_____

_____

_____

_____

_____

DAY 5

There should never be anything you have to hide from your spouse. You and everything you do should be an open book to them.

•••

You should be someone your spouse can completely trust 100% with no reservation. There should be nothing in the dark corners of your mind that aren't brought out into the light before your spouse and God. There should be nothing that you feel needs to be hidden and if there is, it's probably because Satan has convinced you that it should be because breakthrough is on the other side of your honesty. The truth isn't always easy to accept or to confess... but it is always worth it. Let today be the day that if there is anything hidden, it is brought into the light. Ask God to lead you and help you live a life with no secrecy in your marriage. Gut level honesty brings a sense of freedom to be who you are and to feel accepted and loved.

•••

Then I acknowledged my sin to you and did not cover up iniquity. I said, "I will confess my transgressions to the Lord." And you for gave the guilt of my sin.
Psalm 32:5 (NIV)

Thoughts and ideas:

_____

_____

_____

_____

_____

_____

_____

_____

_____

_____

_____

_____

_____

_____

_____

_____

_____

_____

_____

_____

_____

DAY 6

One thing we have learned is that it is really fun to be super silly with each other. To laugh and to cause laughter. But most of all to choose joy when Satan is screaming the opposite.

•••

Today is the day to dance in the kitchen. To go on a walk and call a race to the next stop sign. To have fun. Today is the day to choose joy. Satan is always trying to get us offended, fearful, stressed out, worried, and anything else he can that will pull us away from enjoying time with our spouse. But it is so necessary as children of God to rest in His promises and enjoy every day life. God is good, and we can count on Him to take care of things that we can't. Choose joy today because your hope is in God. Don't look at circumstances, look at your spouse and most of all look at your God. Remember that today is a blessing and make it a good one.

Choose joy today. Choose. Choose. Choose.

•••

Clap your hands, all you nations; shout to God with cries of joy.
Psalm 47:1 (NIV)

Thoughts and ideas:

_____

_____

_____

_____

_____

_____

_____

_____

_____

_____

_____

_____

_____

_____

_____

_____

_____

_____

_____

DAY 7

If you can't think of a single reason to stay with your spouse, remember that Jesus went to the cross for you when you were useless to him. He kept his covenant with you and you didn't give Him a single reason to.

•••

Do you feel like your marriage is hanging on by its last strand? Like the rope that once held you together has unraveled, and you are not sure how much longer it will hold? Despite what you may think or what Satan may be telling you, it is not a lost cause! We serve a God of restoration and redemption. Stop looking at that unraveled rope and gaze upon our miracle working God. If there are people in your life speaking negatively over your marriage and pointing your attention to the unraveled rope, it's time to remind them and yourself that if Jesus can resurrect a dead person, He can resurrect a dead marriage. God loves you and He loves your marriage. He longs to see unity in your marriage even more than you do. Your marriage is not a joke to Him and is not something He takes lightly. Hang in there and cling to God's word and His faithfulness. He is fighting for your marriage.

•••

He went in and said to them, "Why all this commotion and wailing? The child is not dead but asleep." But they laughed at him. After he put them all out, he took the child's father and mother and the disciples who were with him, and went in where the child was. He took her by the hand and said to her, "Talitha koum!" (which means "Little girl, I say to you, get up!"). Immediately the girl stood up and began to walk around (she was twelve years old). At this they were completely astonished.
Mark 5:39-42 (NIV)

Thoughts and ideas:

_____

_____

_____

_____

_____

_____

_____

_____

_____

_____

_____

_____

_____

_____

_____

_____

_____

_____

_____

_____

DAY 8

It is not like Christ to keep bringing up mistakes and failures from the past… It is however, like Satan.

•••

Jesus takes delight in you. He loves you. His mercies are new every morning. He embraces today with you. Satan, however, reminds you of all the times you've messed up. He tries to haunt you with the past. He brings up your mistakes and tries to make you feel ashamed and unworthy… It is so important to ask yourself, who are you reflecting in your marriage? Are you embracing today with your spouse? Or are you focused on what went wrong yesterday? Ask God each morning to help you reflect His love and forgiveness in your marriage.

•••

The steadfast love of the Lord never ceases; his mercies never come to an end; they are new every morning; great is your faithfulness.
Lamentations 3:22-23 (ESV)

Thoughts and ideas:

_____

_____

_____

_____

_____

_____

_____

_____

_____

_____

_____

_____

_____

_____

_____

_____

_____

_____

_____

_____

DAY 9

Compliment your spouse every day.

•••

Flood your spouse with compliments. Publicly and privately build them up. Let them know that you are focused on and that you see the best in them. It will not only edify them but watch how it does the same for you. We are personally big fans of compliments in our own marriage. It just feels good to be complimented, and also to compliment. For instance, if you wake up and you think your spouse is looking good, tell them. If your spouse cooks an awesome dinner, let them know how good it tasted. If your spouse does something to your home that makes it look a little homier, tell them how they added such a nice touch. If your spouse works hard to provide for your family, let people know that you are so thankful for their hard work. If your spouse has great integrity, let them know how proud you are of them for that characteristic. Complements are refreshing. And we don't believe that you can give too many!

•••

You are altogether beautiful, my darling; there is no flaw in you.
Song of Songs 4:7 (NIV)

Thoughts and ideas:

_____

_____

_____

_____

_____

_____

_____

_____

_____

_____

_____

_____

_____

_____

_____

_____

_____

_____

_____

_____

DAY 10

When you hurt your spouse you hurt Christ, too.
•••

Think of someone you love unconditionally. How would you feel if someone was rude or harsh towards them? Not happy, right? It would probably hurt you, too, huh? You know that's exactly how God feels about your spouse? That's His child you're dealing with and it hurts Him when they are hurt or treated wrongly. That is such a huge form of accountability in our marriage, personally. I love God so much that it moves me to love and respect my spouse even when it is a choice I have to make rather than just a natural reaction. If the way you love God does not change the way that you love your spouse, then I wonder how much you love either of them? Ask God to help you reflect love to your spouse in reverence to your love for Him.
•••

"And one of them struck the servant of the high priest, cutting off his right ear. But Jesus answered, "No more of this!" And he touched the man's ear and healed him."
Luke 22:50-51 (NIV)

Thoughts and ideas:

_____

_____

_____

_____

_____

_____

_____

_____

_____

_____

_____

_____

_____

_____

_____

_____

_____

_____

_____

_____

DAY 11

If I have learned one thing about getting along with my spouse, it is that Jesus treats me the way that my spouse wants to be treated by me.

•••

Your spouse isn't perfect, and it's so important to realize that neither are you. It's so easy to forget all the times we've messed up when our spouse messes up once. That's why it is so important to remember the value of your marriage over the frustration of a moment. Take a minute to remember the way Jesus treats you when you mess up. He doesn't panic or freak out or yell, He points you back to the cross and reminds you that He still loves you. It is vital to our marriages to forgive, to remember how much we've been forgiven for, and to cling ever so tightly to the example of Jesus when it comes to the way we treat our spouse. Ask God for guidance and grace when it comes to loving your spouse the way you are called to. He is willing and able to help you every step of the way!

•••

Whenever you stand praying, if you have anything against anyone, forgive him [drop the issue, let it go], so that your Father who is in heaven will also forgive you your transgressions and wrongdoings [against Him and others].
Mark 11:25 (AMP)

Thoughts and ideas:

_____

_____

_____

_____

_____

_____

_____

_____

_____

_____

_____

_____

_____

_____

_____

_____

_____

_____

_____

_____

_____

_____

DAY 12

Nothing can wreak havoc in your marriage unless it is given more thought than prayer and more attention than Jesus.

•••

It seems like so many times the attention we put on a problem turns out to be a bigger problem than what we thought the actual problem was. How many times have you been so worried or stressed out about something, just for it to work out fine? I know I do that all the time. I get so worked up about how we're gonna pay this or that, or how we're gonna make it to two different places at once, and then it works out fine. Why do things seem to work out fine? Because I am a child of God and while I was freaking out, God was sorting things out for me. He had a plan for my problem. He had an answer for my anxiety. As children of God, we have no reason to stress or worry. As children of the Creator of time itself, we can trust His timing. As Children of the King of kings, worrying is wasted time. We are covered. We are held. We are cared for. We are loved. We have an almighty God that is willing and able to intercede for us in any circumstance or situation and work it out for our good. If there is something in your marriage that is sucking the life out your joy, if there is something in your marriage that has set up a roadblock in your hope, speak truth over those things right now in Jesus name! It's just a matter of time! God is for you! He has a plan! He has a purpose! He is good! He is faithful! Trust Him!

•••

Since you are my rock and my fortress, for the sake of your name lead and guide me. Keep me from the trap that is set for me, for you are my refuge.
Psalm 31:3-4 (NIV)

Thoughts and ideas:

_____

_____

_____

_____

_____

_____

_____

_____

_____

_____

_____

_____

_____

_____

_____

_____

_____

_____

_____

_____

DAY 13

Give your spouse someone they can count on and trust.

•••

One way you can reflect God in your marriage is to keep your promises. God doesn't break his promises based on your behavior and you shouldn't break yours based on your spouse's behavior. Look to God and ask him to help you be a vow honoring spouse and protect you against any lie that Satan tries to tell you. He will always attempt to pull you away from the words that you said on your wedding day when the "worse" rolls around. But you said for better or worse. Be determined to show your spouse that you meant that.

•••

For it is written: "Be holy, because I am holy."
1 Peter 1:16 (NIV)

Thoughts and ideas:

_____

_____

_____

_____

_____

_____

_____

_____

_____

_____

_____

_____

_____

_____

_____

_____

_____

_____

_____

DAY 14

The best thing I can do for my marriage is focus on God and His word.

•••

I read this analogy one time that was talking about how what was inside is what will come out. They explained it using a coffee mug... They started out asking this question, "If you were holding a coffee mug full of coffee and someone bumped into you, causing you to spill it... Why did you spill coffee?" The answer was that you spilled the coffee because there was coffee and your mug... Had there been hot chocolate, you would have spilled hot chocolate. Whatever was in the mug, is what you would have spilled out. The analogy ended with this question, "So if life comes and shakes you... What will spill out? What's in your mug?" That is such a good analogy. If you are consistently filling your mug with good and godly things, if you are persistent about getting God's word into your system, your marriage will be built on solid ground. Because those are the things that will surface when a storm shakes you.

•••

Above all else, guard your heart, for everything you do flows from it.
Proverbs 4:23(NIV)

A good man brings good things out of the good stored up in him, and an evil man brings evil things out of the evil stored up in him.
Matthew 12:35 (NIV)

Thoughts and ideas:

_____

_____

_____

_____

_____

_____

_____

_____

_____

_____

_____

_____

_____

_____

_____

_____

_____

_____

_____

_____

_____

_____

DAY 15

"I still love you." That's the character of God.

•••

No matter what happened yesterday. No matter what was said or what was silent. No matter if forgiveness was sought after or not. His mercies are new every morning. He is always ready to forgive. Not based on your character, but because that is His character. That's the example He set for us. He is always willing to forgive and show us mercy. That's the example we are to follow.

•••

Be kind and compassionate to one another, forgiving each other, just as in Christ God for gave you.
Ephesians. 4:32 (NIV)

Thoughts and ideas:

_____

_____

_____

_____

_____

_____

_____

_____

_____

_____

_____

_____

_____

_____

_____

_____

_____

_____

_____

_____

DAY 16

The best kind of marriage is the kind where Yesterdays frustrations do not affect the quality of today.

•••

So many times, I've had to remind myself to, "pick your battles." I say that in my head quite often. When Satan or even my own flesh try to get me flustered about something that was done yesterday or something that was said months ago. Sometimes it is so tempting to bring up the past, but it is so not worth it. Not only because it puts a strain on our marriage but also because God never does that to me. Another thing I ask myself pretty often is, "Is it worth it?" Is it worth it to rob the moment or even the day of its joy because I am still thinking about that time_____. (You can fill in the blank.) No, it's not worth it. That's one of those moments to let go and let God. That's one of those moments to ask God to help me get that off of my mind and out of my system and focus on all of the beauty and blessings I have with my spouse. That's one of those moments to use my authority to tell Satan to get away from me in the name of Jesus and to remind him that he will not have his way in my marriage. Do not use the past as ammunition, leave it where it is... in the past. Thank God for today and show your spouse how thankful you are that you get to spend it with them.

•••

I consider that our present sufferings are not worth comparing with the glory that will be revealed in us.
Romans 8:18 (NIV)

Thoughts and ideas:

_____

_____

_____

_____

_____

_____

_____

_____

_____

_____

_____

_____

_____

_____

_____

_____

_____

_____

_____

_____

_____

DAY 17

If you think your spouse is your biggest problem, then go take a look in the mirror.

•••

Your spouse is never your biggest problem. It's that voice that may tell you that they are. Or that voice that may whisper that you'd be happier with someone else or better off alone. Or that voice that may whisper that your situation gives you the right to sin. Do not be deceived. Ask God to align your thoughts with His word and His purpose for your marriage. Tell Satan to go to Hell and speak life over your marriage. Tell him he does not belong around you and he is not welcome in your marriage. Tell him to get out of your home and go back to his own.

•••

Many are the afflictions of the righteous, but the Lord delivers him out of them all.
Psalm 34:19 (ESV)

Thoughts and ideas:

_____

_____

_____

_____

_____

_____

_____

_____

_____

_____

_____

_____

_____

_____

_____

_____

_____

_____

_____

_____

DAY 18

Don't treat your spouse the way that they treat you, treat your spouse the way that God treats you.

•••

Do you want your marriage to be beautiful? To feel like a breath of fresh air? To radiate love, joy, peace, and kindness? We believe that there is a way to have that… We believe that is the kind of marriage that is produced when a *husband and a wife decide* that their marriage has to be less about themselves, their feelings, and their desires and centrally based on Jesus. Based on reflecting His patience and character. Based on pleasing Him. Based on shining a light for His kingdom. When God's love shapes the way you love your spouse rather than your spouses actions shaping the way that you love them, your marriage will be radiant.

•••

Those who look to him are radiant; their faces are never covered with shame. Psalm 34:5 (NIV)

Thoughts and ideas:

_____

_____

_____

_____

_____

_____

_____

_____

_____

_____

_____

_____

_____

_____

_____

_____

_____

_____

_____

DAY 19

You cannot control your spouse, so you must work at controlling yourself.

•••

We believe that one of the leading causes (if not the leading cause) of divorce is the lack of self-control. Not choosing to walk according to God's word but rather choosing to stumble according to the flesh. It's selfishness. It's an internal decision that the way you feel is more important than the truth of God's word. You can't make your spouse's decisions, but you can make your own and you can choose your reactions! Put less focus on trying to fix your spouse, and more on not allowing their decisions to waiver your commitment to Jesus. One of the best ways to influence your spouse to make godly decisions is by making godly decisions for yourself.

•••

A man without self-control is like a city broken into and left without walls.
Proverbs 25:28 (ESV)

Thoughts and ideas:

_____

_____

_____

_____

_____

_____

_____

_____

_____

_____

_____

_____

_____

_____

_____

_____

_____

_____

_____

_____

_____

DAY 20

You will never be happy in your marriage until you choose to focus on God rather than all the things that bother you.

•••

Whew y'all… it's so true that sometimes we tend to focus on the negative. How our spouse said they would do something and then they forgot. How they said they would pay a bill and now there's a late fee. Things happen, fingers are pointed, and then everyone is flustered. However, crying over spilt milk doesn't clean it up or change the fact that it was spilt. Making it a habit of showing grace rather than grumbling will result in a lot more peace in your marriage. Learn from mistakes, have a conversation about them if it is necessary, but don't dwell on them. Turn your attention to God and ask him to help you show grace to your spouse the way that He shows grace to you.

•••

Set your minds on things above, not on earthly things.
Colossians 3:2 (NIV)

Thoughts and ideas:

_____

_____

_____

_____

_____

_____

_____

_____

_____

_____

_____

_____

_____

_____

_____

_____

_____

_____

_____

DAY 21

I hope you've prayed for your spouse more times than you've gotten frustrated at them this week.

•••

When we were at our worst, Jesus prayed for us. When our sin had Jesus crucified, He looked up to heaven and said, "Father, forgive them, for they do not know what they are doing (Luke 23:34)." Can we just close our eyes and take ten seconds to soak that in? You guys, that's love. He could've been mad, he could've cursed us, he could have climbed off of that cross... but He didn't. He prayed for us. Why? Because He loves us. He has a covenant with us that means more to Him than our sinful choices. He didn't lash out at us and tell us how bad we are or how much we had just messed up, He prayed for us. This. This is the most faithful display of love. When your spouse frustrates you... how do you react? I think we can all work on trying to react a little more like Jesus. With prayer. God help us! Amen!

Ask God to help you in times of frustration to reflect Jesus.

•••

For the eyes of the Lord are [looking favorably] upon the righteous (the upright), and His ears are attentive to their prayer (eager to answer), but the face of the Lord is against those who practice evil.
1 Peter 3:12 (AMP)

Thoughts and ideas:

_____

_____

_____

_____

_____

_____

_____

_____

_____

_____

_____

_____

_____

_____

_____

_____

_____

_____

_____

DAY 22

Take time to understand and communicate before you waste time misunderstanding and miscommunicating.

•••

It is so easy to fall into the pit of a misunderstanding. We've done this so many times. It's like you get offended by something that was said or done just because you didn't take time to understand. This happened for us very often when our baby was a newborn. It was like we were trying to correct each other constantly on how to handle her only to soon realize that was not benefiting our marriage in the least bit. Quite the opposite, actually. It was only leading to offense after offense. With that, we had to have a conversation about how we realized what was going on and that it had to stop. The reality was that we were just trying to help each other, but at the same time not taking time to understand that we were both brand new at parenting and both trying to figure things out. After we had that conversation, we began to see God start working in our marriage for the better… if there is something going on in your marriage that is causing offense after offense. Take time today to have a conversation. It could just be a misunderstanding.

•••

Dear children, let us not love with words or speech but with actions and in truth.
1John 3:18 (NIV)

Thoughts and ideas:

_____

_____

_____

_____

_____

_____

_____

_____

_____

_____

_____

_____

_____

_____

_____

_____

_____

_____

_____

DAY 23

God, please protect us from anything that could compromise our relationship with you our spouse.

•••

Can you think of a time where something that shouldn't have happened wouldn't have happened had you not put yourself in a situation for it to? I can think of many of those times for myself. Sometimes there are things that can easily be avoided just by simply avoiding a person, place, or thing. However, it is so important that we ask God for guidance. Ask God to help you avoid people, places, and things that wouldn't honor your spouse and more importantly your love for Jesus and your thankfulness for the cross. Do not compromise your relationship with your spouse or with God for something that Satan has dressed in temporary satisfaction that in reality is just heartbreak.

•••

You are my hiding place; you will protect me from trouble and surround me with songs of deliverance.
Psalm 32:7 (NIV)

Thoughts and ideas:

_____

_____

_____

_____

_____

_____

_____

_____

_____

_____

_____

_____

_____

_____

_____

_____

_____

_____

_____

_____

DAY 24

Your relationship with your spouse should not shape your relationship with God... But your relationship with God should shape your relationship with your spouse.

•••

How often do you stop and take a second to reflect before you react? How often to you pause to pray before you panic? As Christians, it is so important that we don't just dive headfirst into our feelings, because sometimes the way we feel doesn't lead us to saying or doing godly things. For the sake of our love for God and our marriages, it is so important to take a minute to align our hearts and thoughts with God's word so that we can respond to situations in ways that glorify Jesus. We need to start asking God more often to make our hearts so in tune with Him that our actions follow His example and our thoughts are fixed on His ways. The more we focus on God, the more beautiful our marriages will be.

•••

But the fruit of the Spirit is love, joy, peace, forbearance, kindness, goodness, faithfulness, gentleness and self-control. Galatians 5:22 (NIV)

Thoughts and ideas:

_____

_____

_____

_____

_____

_____

_____

_____

_____

_____

_____

_____

_____

_____

_____

_____

_____

_____

DAY 25

Today is a good day to choose a good day.

•••

Sometimes good days don't just come naturally. The morning is hectic, someone gets a flat tire, the power gets cut off, etc. Sometimes things happen that literally make us feel like the whole day is just awful. However, that doesn't have to be the case! It does have to be a choice, though. Sometimes we are put in positions where we can either have a bad attitude about an unfortunate event, or we can thank God for all the blessings in our lives. Today is a good day to choose a good day. Not based on how the day goes but based on the fact that God has been so good to you. Make today the day that you start trying to focus on your blessings rather than your circumstances.

•••

May the God of hope fill you with all joy and peace as you trust in him, so that you may overflow with hope by the power of the Holy Spirit.
Romans 15:13 (NIV)

Thoughts and ideas:

_____

_____

_____

_____

_____

_____

_____

_____

_____

_____

_____

_____

_____

_____

_____

_____

_____

_____

_____

DAY 26

Even if your spouse isn't doing as they should, you still should.
•••
One time I was at conference and the speaker was talking about how they had been in a dry season and were having a hard time hearing the voice of God. They said that while they were in that season, since they weren't sure what steps to take next or what direction God was calling them in, the only thing they knew to do was to continue living according to God's word. To wake up every day in that season and say, "God, I give this day to you. Help me to live in a way that glorifies You." I thought that was so powerful. That when we don't know what to do, we can simply just do what is right. We can just continue to be faithful with our every moment. I love how the sermon ended, too. They said that in that season, one day they woke up and heard God so clearly say, "It's over." That day that season ended, and God started to take them in such a clear direction. Sometimes we go through seasons that aren't fun, that aren't enjoyable, and that are just down right hard… but, we are still called to be faithful in the waiting. If you're in one of those seasons, while you wait, just submit yourself to God, and choose to do the right thing.
•••
Let us not become weary in doing good, for at the proper time we will reap a harvest if we do not give up.
Galatians 6:9 (NIV)

Thoughts and ideas:

_____

_____

_____

_____

_____

_____

_____

_____

_____

_____

_____

_____

_____

_____

_____

_____

_____

DAY 27

God, if I ever stop seeing my spouse the way that you do...
Please take my hands off of my eyes.

•••

Sometimes it's easy to see our spouse for the things they do rather than who they are. It's easier to see their weaknesses than it is to see their strengths. It's easier to see their stumbles than it is to see their strides. However, that is the opposite of how God looks at us. He sees us through the eyes of love. He sees the best in us, even in our worst seasons. He is our biggest fan. He is our greatest friend. The way He looks at us is how we should strive to see our spouse. An encourager, not a nagger. A forgiver, not one to hold a grudge. He is for us, not against us.

•••

Therefore, if anyone is in Christ, he is a new creation. The old has passed away; behold, the new has come.
2 Corinthians 5:17 (ESV)

Thoughts and ideas:

_____

_____

_____

_____

_____

_____

_____

_____

_____

_____

_____

_____

_____

_____

_____

_____

_____

_____

_____

_____

DAY 28

You may not have went into your marriage expecting it to turn out the way it is, but God did. Talk to Him about it.

•••

Have you ever expected to go into something and it to go one way, yet it went the opposite? As much as I hope that isn't your marriage, if it is, you are not alone. I think this happens to a lot of people. You go into marriage so giddy and head over heels… that honeymoon stage is so fun. Then you get into a rhythm and the reality of work, family, and many other things add into the mix. You get comfortable and some of the things that once made you so excited have seemed to fade out? That's a normal place, but don't settle for that. Ask God to restore that excitement, ask Him to show you new ways to bless your spouse, ask God to bring your marriage to its full potential and use you in any way that He can. Maybe it's time to let some things go that were said or done in the past. Ask God to help you get rid of any filth that has built up in your mind that is keeping you from the intimacy you once had. God is willing and able to restore, you just have to decide not to settle for less.

•••

How abundant are the good things that you have stored up for those who fear you, that you bestow in the sight of all, on those who take refuge in you.
Psalm 31:19 (NIV)

Thoughts and ideas:

_____

_____

_____

_____

_____

_____

_____

_____

_____

_____

_____

_____

_____

_____

_____

_____

_____

_____

_____

DAY 29

The most contagious thing that you will ever bring home to your family is your attitude. Make sure you are spreading something in your home that Jesus doesn't have to heal.

•••

We cannot afford to run out of patience before we see our spouse. We cannot afford to run out of grace before we see our spouse. We cannot afford to not be kind. We cannot afford to be snappy. We can't afford to refuse to be affectionate. Why? Because those are the things that Satan is selling, and they will make your marriage go bankrupt. It is so important to bring home a good attitude to your spouse. It is so important that your spouse is not getting your leftovers. It is so important to reflect Jesus. Jesus is the easiest person to live with, so the more we become like Him, the more our home becomes a place of refuge and peace. Decide today that you are more than a conqueror through Christ and you can overcome a bad attitude for the sake of your marriage!

•••

Love is patient, love is kind. It does not envy, it does not boast, it is not proud. It does not dishonor others, it is not self-seeking, it is not easily angered, it keeps no record of wrongs. Love does not delight in evil but rejoices with the truth. It always protects, always trusts, always hopes, always perseveres. Love never fails.
1 Corinthians 13:4-9 (NIV)

Thoughts and ideas:

_____

_____

_____

_____

_____

_____

_____

_____

_____

_____

_____

_____

_____

_____

_____

_____

_____

_____

DAY 30

It is not your job to fix your marriage. It is your job to love your spouse even when your marriage seems broken.

•••

Sometimes it would be so easy when things get hard to just put your phone on silent, get in the car, and drive off. The reason we would never encourage that is because that gives Satan room to put your spouse in a state of torment. However, sometimes it is very important, when things get hard, to seclude yourself. To ask your spouse if you can just have a ten-minute break to get alone with Jesus. Jesus shows us how important that is many times in the Bible. He got away to pray. He got away to have time with God alone and give God room to speak. When there are broken moments, days, and even seasons in your marriage... put your attention on God and not on fixing your marriage. The key to a broken marriage is not your marriage being fixed, but your thoughts being fixed. Cling to God's promises in the midst of confusion and what may seem like chaos and give God room to shape you and mold you through it. Maybe the real project God is working on not your marriage, but you.

•••

And we know that in all things God works for the good of those who love him, who have been called according to his purpose. Romans 8:28 (NIV)

Thoughts and ideas:

DAY 31

To be happily married, you must divorce pride, insecurities, impatience, the past, anger, bitterness, sin, and resentment many many times... But never your spouse.

•••

You guys, Satan is called the great deceiver not because he is great in any way but because he has been in the game for a long time. He knows when to step out and when to stand still. He is like a lion, prowling, lurking, waiting for a vulnerable moment to devour your marriage. It is so important to know that your marriage is on Satan's hit list. Your marriage has a target on it. He hates you. He hates your marriage. And he hates God's plan for your marriage. That is why it is so important to be intentional about standing on the word of God! We as God's army always have to be on guard. We must be prepared to fight. We must call on the name of Jesus! We must lay our marriages in His hands! Because though our enemy is out for us, he is no match for our God. However, it's up to us to cling to God through the valley or to fall for Satan's falsified joy ride to the mountain top that leads to regret and heartbreak. Choose Jesus.

•••

And call upon me in the day of trouble; I will deliver you, and you shall glorify me.
Psalm 50:15 (ESV)

Thoughts and ideas:

_____

_____

_____

_____

_____

_____

_____

_____

_____

_____

_____

_____

_____

_____

_____

_____

_____

_____

_____

_____

24556641R00073

Made in the USA
San Bernardino, CA
06 February 2019